The House

The Plane

The Homestead

Mitzi's

Ned's Caravan

The Windmill

the KOALA BROTHERS™

Lolly Comes to Town

Ladybird

6

The outback is full of wonderful sounds – but none is more wonderful than the sound of an ice cream van on a hot, sunny day. And Lolly's ice cream is the best for miles around!

One sweltering afternoon, Alice, Archie and Mitzi were all feeling hot and bothered down by the waterhole. Suddenly, they heard the gentle, jingling, jangling sound of distant music.

TYNDALE
CHRISTIAN SCHOOL

"It's Lolly!" yelled Mitzi.

Sure enough, Lolly's ice cream van soon came into sight. But as it trundled towards the waterhole, no one noticed its engine was making a scraping, scratching, rumbling noise...

"Hi everyone!" Lolly called. "I've been driving through the outback for weeks. Lovely to have someone to talk to!" she grinned. "Anybody for an ice cream?"

"Rather!" said Archie. "What a treat!"

"Yes, please!" beamed Alice.

The friends all agreed that ice cream on a boiling hot day was just the thing to cool them down.

"I hope she's got chocolate-chip," said Mitzi dreamily.

Meanwhile, at the Koala Brothers' homestead, Ned and Buster had found other ways to keep cool. Ned sat in front of a fan, while Buster placed a towel full of ice cubes on his hot head.

Then Frank appeared with a jug of ice-cold orange squash.

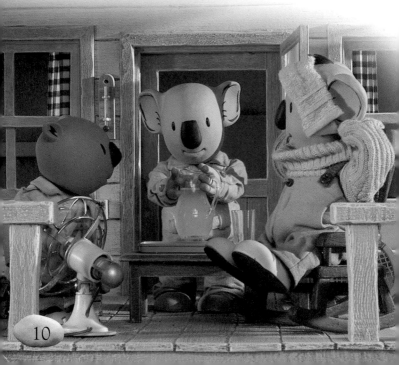

"Thanks, Frank! Just what I need!" said Buster happily. He thought the drink was just for him – and drank down the lot in a few thirsty gulps!

"But... but that was for *all* of us!" gasped Frank.

"Oh, no!" cried Buster, realising his mistake. "I'm sorry. Here, Ned, you can have my ice pack!"

Ned wasn't sure it really suited him.

Back at the waterhole, Lolly leaned
out of her van to give Mitzi a
beautiful, big ice cream cone. It was
filled with chocolate-chip ice cream!

"Oh, thank you Lolly!" said Mitzi.
But just as she took it – BANG!
The ice cream van's engine went
up in smoke! Mitzi jumped in
surprise, and her ice cream fell
SPLAT onto the sizzling sand.

"My ice cream van – it's broken down!" wailed Lolly. She tried turning on the engine again, but it wouldn't start. "The engine keeps the ice cream cold. All my ice cream will melt! What am I going to do?"

Everyone wanted to help, but what could they do? Sammy was good with engines, but he wasn't around.

"I know!" beamed Alice. "I'll drive over to the homestead and get help from Frank and Buster!"

Everyone agreed it was a great idea.
Alice swiftly jumped on her scooter
and scooted away, leaving Archie to
fiddle with the broken engine.

"We've got to think of some way
to stop the ice cream melting,"
said Lolly.

"We could eat it!" cried Mitzi.

Archie frowned. "You can't eat
a whole tub of ice cream!"

Mitzi smiled. "I CAN!"

Alice soon arrived at the
homestead. But, being so forgetful,
she found she wasn't quite sure
why she'd come!

"Maybe if you sit down and
cool off you'll remember,"
suggested Buster.

Alice sat on the veranda next to
Ned. "Why are you wearing that
towel on your head?" she laughed.

"It's an ice pack," said Buster proudly. "Buster made it to cool me down."

"Ice!" cried Alice. She jumped up and danced about with excitement. "That's it! Ice! ICE CREAM!"

Now Alice remembered everything.
She turned to the Koala Brothers.
"Lolly's van has broken down at
the waterhole and her ice cream's
melting!" she said. "She needs
your help!"

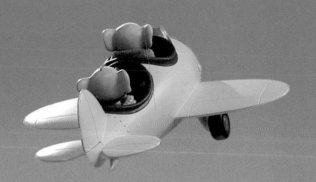

"Leave it to us, Alice," said Frank confidently. He turned to Buster and Ned. "Get ready for take off!"

Frank and Buster buckled up and Ned opened the gate. Soon, it was chocks away! The yellow plane soared up into the wide, blue sky.

Back at the waterhole, the ice cream was still melting – and there was no sign of the Koala Brothers.

Then Mitzi pointed up into the sky. "Look!" she yelled. "They're here!"

The moment the plane had landed, Frank and Buster leapt out. "Don't worry, Lolly," said Frank. "Give me the ice cream."

Lolly passed him the heavy tub. "What are you going to do with it, Frank?" she asked.

"I'm going to fly back to the homestead and freeze the ice cream in our freezer," he said. "There's not a minute to lose!"

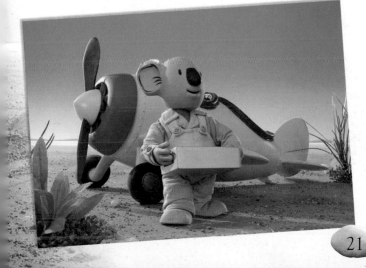

"What about me, Frank?"
asked Buster.

"You can stay here, Buster, and
try to fix the van!" Frank called.

"You Koala Brothers really are
wonderful!" said Lolly happily.

Buster grinned. "We're here
to help!"

Once Frank had flown
away, Buster busied himself
under the bonnet. But it
was no use. "I can't get
it to work," he sighed.

"I bet Sammy can!" cried Mitzi.
Sammy was a wizard with engines
– and she'd just spotted his three-
wheeled van coming their way!

When Sammy arrived, he unclipped
some cables and wiggled some
wires, and Lolly's engine started!

"It worked!" laughed Lolly.
"Thank you Buster and Sammy!"

Buster smiled. "Let's head to the
homestead to get the ice cream!"

Mitzi nodded eagerly. "I can't wait for my chocolate-chip!"

Back at the homestead, Frank had some *very* good news for Lolly.

"The ice cream's fine!" he grinned.

Lolly was quite overcome with happiness. "Oh Frank!" she spluttered, as her friends gathered round her. "How can I thank you... How can I possibly thank you all?"

Mitzi took a couple of steps forward and smiled shyly. "Well..."

Lolly laughed. "Ha! Ha! Ha! I know – WHO'S FOR ICE CREAM?"

Everyone cheered. "YES!"

"Mine's a chocolate-chip!" shouted Mitzi.

When Lolly had finished handing
out ice creams, it was time for her
to go.

"Bye, Lolly!" everyone called.
"Thank you!"

Lolly leaned out the van window
and beamed at them all. "I'll be
back soon!" she promised.

And everyone hoped that she *would* be back soon. Because on a hot and sunny day in the outback, the most magical sound of all was the sound of Lolly's ice cream van as it came to town.

The General Store

Alice's House

Post Office

The Post